# My Gift to the World

by Lizette Geisler

Illustrated by Carol Timpone

My Dedications

To Dad, my amazing, loving father, who has supported and believed in *my* "Gift to the World." You live forever in my heart and soul. I love you!

To God and my Angels-
Thank you for divinely guiding me and showing me the way.

-Lizette Geisler

Illustrations by Carol Timpone

To my husband Jim, who has always supported my art, my son Michael, my best critic, and my daughters Amy, Melissa and Katie, for always encouraging me.

-Carol Timpone

It's my gift to the world.

What do you mean,
"my gift to the world"?

It's something you give
or do that will help someone's life.

I help children learn how to play the piano
and make beautiful music.

Some people are naturally quite
creative or imaginative – they could
be musicians, artists, make
TV commercials or
magazine advertisements,
or own their own business.

Other people are good at fixing things.
They could help people by becoming plumbers, computer
technicians, physical therapists or car mechanics.

Some people are great at building things and putting things together - carpenters and construction workers, architects, engineers, and computer assemblers.

Then, there are some people who are athletic, great
at sports or dancing - soccer players, football
players, ballerinas, gymnasts, and people in
so many other sports!

Some people are great with people - they seem to have a gift for understanding others, and can talk to everyone and make many friends wherever they go! They could be counselors, teachers, work within the community or help companies interact with the public better.

Others are great writers. They could be newspaper journalists, write a screenplay, or write a book.

Some people are mathematical and logical – they are great with numbers and figuring things out – they have a gift for seeing the details in everything – scientists, doctors, business accountants and lawyers use this gift.

There are so many gifts we each have!
But knowing them is one of the most
important discoveries you can make!

Because then you can create your own way to
give your gifts to the world!

Mom, how did you know that teaching piano was your gift to the world?

I knew, Valentina,
because it made me
feel very good inside.
It makes you happy to give
your gift to the world . . .
but even more . . .

When you give your special gift to someone, . . . .

. . . it helps them, and it puts a smile on their face, too!

Aa Bb Cc Dd Ee Ff Gg H h I i Jj Kk L

Valentina, think of your teacher, Ms. B. Her gift to the world is teaching children. She teaches you how to learn, so you will come to know the world around you better.

Nn Oo Pp Qq Rr Ss Tt Uu Vv Ww Xx Yy Zz

Ms. B. also helps you learn about yourself,
and teaches you about acting with respect
and dignity toward others.
Teaching, her gift to the world, helps children
become better human beings.

A person's gift to the world is whatever
they love to do that makes a positive
difference in someone else's life.

**Oh!** You mean like my doctor. His gift to the world is helping people feel better!

Yes! Your doctor loves helping kids feel better, by taking care of them when they're sick or hurt.

And you know, Valentina, we take our dog, Snickers,
to the veterinarian when he is not feeling good.
So, the veterinarian's gift to the world- . . .

. . . is taking care of animals and helping them get better and be healthy.

And he does this because- . . .

. . . he loves happy, healthy animals!

Yes!

# Mom, what gift will I give to the world?

Anything you do with love, Valentina,
is your gift to the world . . .

. . . Anything you do with love.

## Author's Statement to Parents and Teachers

Having taught in both public and private elementary schools for years, and as a contributing author in the book, *It's All About Kids: Every Child Deserves a Teacher of the Year*, I have noticed that at the beginning of the school year, we always talk about what the students want to be when they grow up and what kind of jobs they would like to do. And I began thinking, what is really important are not the jobs that are out there, but how do we best identify and nurture into full blossoming our children's gifts, their unique traits that make them so special?

Every child (and adult) has a unique set of traits and talents,* which I call "gifts." When you are aware of them – either as a parent or a teacher – it will help you guide them toward their purpose in life, what they have the capacity to give to the world as a service, job, or career. We all know that when you give to others what you're naturally good at, your own unique gifts, then you are happy . . . and others will be, too! That's because each person you touch will be able to feel your enthusiasm and passion for life coming through in what you give.

I wanted to write a book in which I could talk to students about the importance of discovering their own unique gifts. *My Gift to the World* will hopefully inspire all children to grow in self-confidence and self-worth, by recognizing we are each blessed with special gifts that expand joy when they are shared with the world!

*Find out more about the distinguished Harvard Professor of Education Dr. Howard Gardner's work with multiple intelligences at www.HowardGardner.com; also, to find out more about the educational applications of multiple intelligences, please go to: http://www.kaganonline.com/catalog/multiple_intelligences.php

www.mygiftstotheworld.com